In memory of my mother who was always there for me,
which was priceless ~ T C

For baby O and Mum ~ T N

LITTLE TIGER PRESS LTD,
an imprint of the Little Tiger Group
1 Coda Studios,
189 Munster Road,
London SW6 6AW
www.littletiger.co.uk

First published in Great Britain 2019

SNEAKY BEAK

Tracey Corderoy

Tony Neal

LITTLE TIGER
LONDON

Bear and Hamster were enjoying their favourite programme,
when suddenly it stopped for an **advert**.
  "Not that **Sneaky Beak** again!" tutted Bear.
"What is it this time . . . ?"

IS YOUR BED

BOUNCY ENOUGH?

Our *Snores-Galore Mega Bed* is the bounciest EVER. Sweet dreams guaranteed every night!

Call for a bounce test on your old bed

NOW!

"A bounce test!" chuckled Bear.
"Oh Hamster, whatever next?!"

But late that night, Bear's head began to whirl . . .

Was that a broken spring?

And was his mattress sagging?

As Hamster snored on, Bear just couldn't sleep.
"**Good gracious me!**" he cried. "What if my bed
ISN'T bouncy enough after all?!"
And he tossed and turned **all night long.**

First thing the next day Bear called for a bounce test, and Sneaky Beak **zoomed** up in a van.

Hello! Trouble sleeping?
That simply won't do!
If you need a new bed,
I've a deal just for you!

His bounce test bunnies got to work.

Then Sneaky Beak checked the report.
"Thank goodness you called, Bear!" he said with a gasp.
"This bed's out of bounce **completely.** You need the
Snores-Galore Mega Bed right away!"

But Bear's new bouncy bed was **enormous.**
There was room for nothing else.
"Wait!" he squeaked as Hamster's things were carted out.
"Sweet dreams!" replied Sneaky Beak. "Oh! But remember:
you'll sleep better after a nice **bubbly bath.**"
He handed Bear a leaflet and was gone.

"A WHAT??!" gulped Bear,
and started to read . . .

**IS YOUR BATH
BUBBLY
ENOUGH?**

Our Super-Whirl
Turbo Tub has it ALL!

Wave machine, bubble-blowers,
jets — and more!

Call **NOW!**

Bear shook his head. "Our old tub
is just fine!" But at bathtime . . .

. . . he wasn't so sure!

"Gosh! What if our bath ISN'T bubbly enough?!" he cried. Uh-oh . . . Bear rang Sneaky Beak at once, who rumbled up in a ten ton truck.

"Hello! Titchy bubbles? That simply won't do! If you need a new bath, I've a deal just for you!

It came with boxfuls of taps and tubes that soon filled the entire bathroom. "Marvellous choice!" Sneaky Beak chirped when at last the job was done.

TURBO

"Ooo! What does this twirly thing do?" wondered Bear. And they soon found out . . .

Next morning, at breakfast, Bear was waiting with a present.
"Here, Hamster! To cheer you up," he said.

"It's a **Crunch-O-Matic**
Granola Maker, see?"

"The thing is," he explained, "I was starting
to worry that our cereal wasn't
CRUNCHY enough!
Don't start the day with a soggy snack -
bring that crunchy goodness back!"

Crunch
-O-
Matic

oats

RAISINS

NUTS

He plugged it in, and Hamster waited
as the oats and raisins softly swirled.
Then with a clunk and a whirr . . .

Hamster's present hadn't cheered him up **AT ALL.**
"We need a holiday,"
Bear said with a sigh.

Then two beady eyes peeped in . . .

Hello!
Feeling glum?
Need a break from
this place? . . .

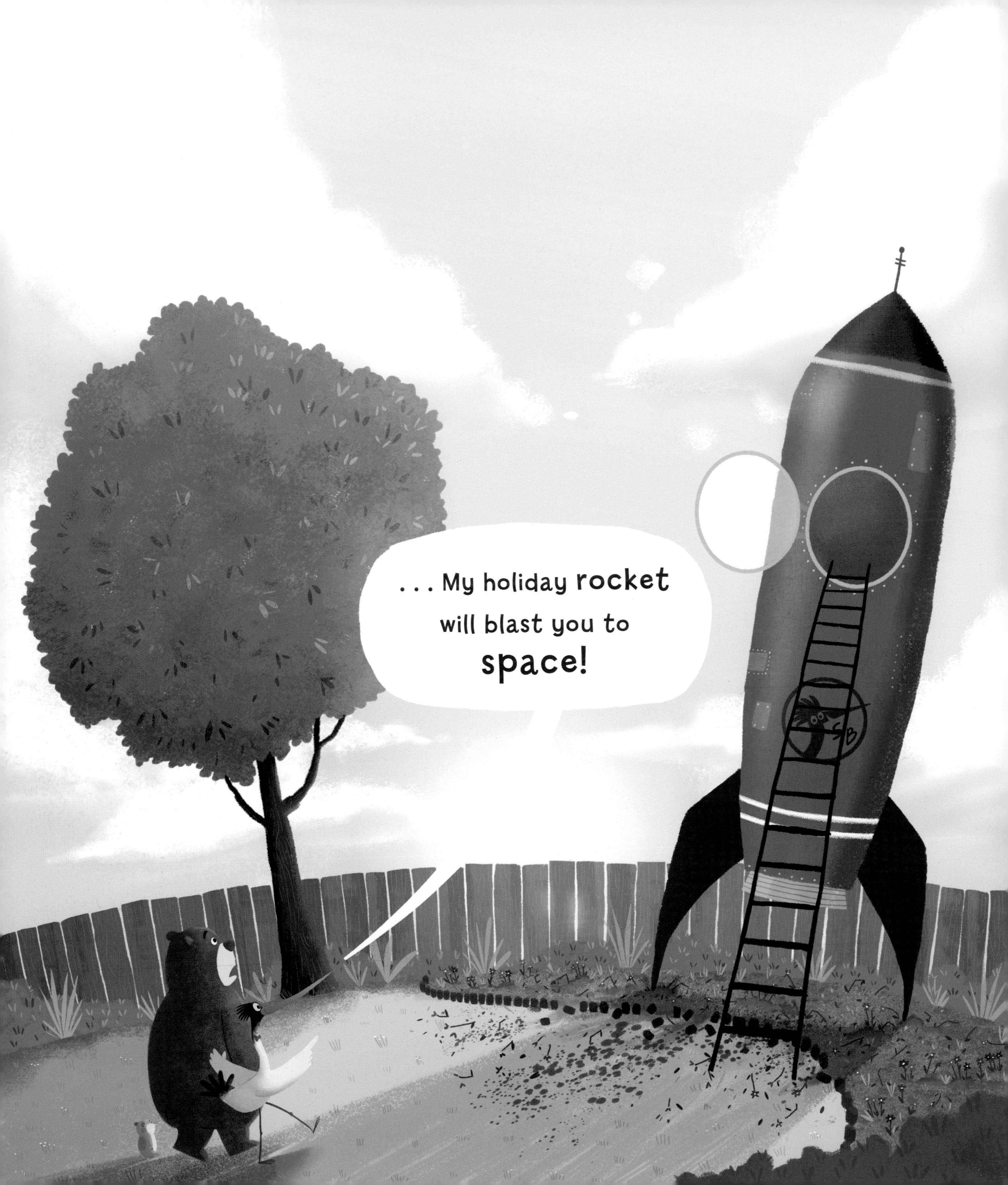
. . . My holiday rocket
will blast you to
space!

In a blink, Bear was whisked up into the rocket.
Then — **ZOOM** — he was soaring through the sky,
while Hamster was getting further and further away.

Outer space was really quiet and calm.
The perfect place to think.

"How silly I've been," whispered Bear,
"changing beds, and bathtubs, and breakfasts."
What made him happiest of all was
none of those things.

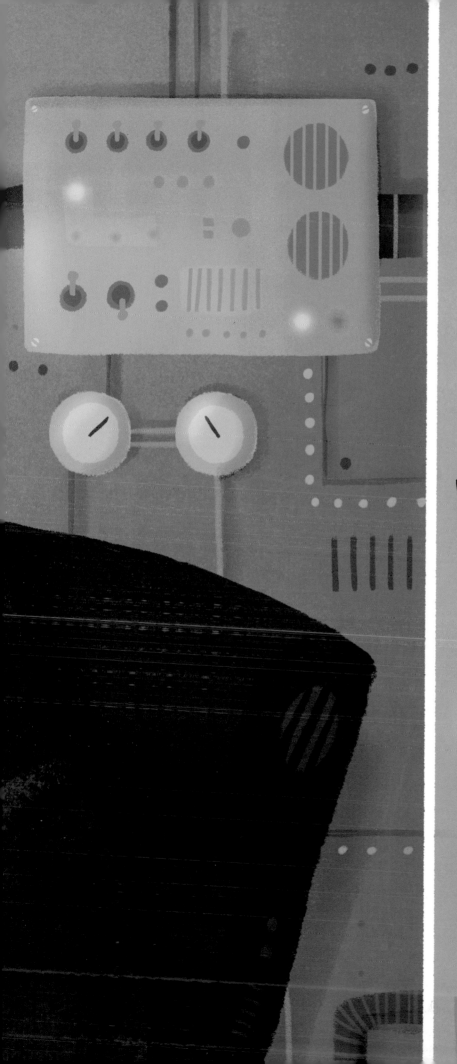

So Bear set the rocket's dial
to take him right back home . . .

SPACE   **HOME**

. . . to the friend he wouldn't change for anything.

"Oh, Hamster!" said Bear.

"I've missed you!"

Bear and Hamster tidied up together.
Their new stuff was just getting in the way.

"The question," said Bear, "is what are we going to **do** with it all?"

With that, a beak poked in through the letterbox.

IS YOUR BIN BIG ENOUGH?
Our new *Trash-tastic Dustbins* will hold **ALL** your unwanted rubbish!

Open your door to test one out **NOW!**

Bear folded his arms.
"No, thanks!" he called back . . .

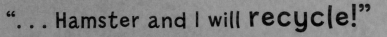

"... Hamster and I will **recycle!**"

From then on, things were simply fine.
Bear and Hamster had each other,
and that was all they needed.

But Sneaky Beak's dustbin did come in rather handy after all!